STALKED BY THE VET

EMMA BRAY

CHAPTER
ONE

Greg

I'M NURSING A BLACK COFFEE, the steam curling up like the slow rise of dawn as I scan the room. The café's a mishmash of chipped mugs and mismatched chairs, and it's got this comforting hum that lets me fade into the wallpaper, unnoticed and unbothered.

My fingers trace the rim of my cup, circling without intent, while my eyes flicker across the room, always watching—habit, I guess.

Then *she* bursts in, a burst of life against the monotony, like a high-definition scene cutting through static.

The door swings open with confidence, and this pretty little brunette struts into the café like she owns the joint. She's a kaleidoscope of color in this drab palette, her vibrant energy impossible to ignore. It's not just the bold prints that wrap around her or the way she moves—like music turned to flesh and bone—it's everything.

She's topped off with a hat, stylish as hell, tilted just so. It's one of those wide-brimmed numbers that scream 'I've got flair' louder than words ever could. Her hair spills out from underneath it, long strands that catch the light and throw it back with a shine.

"Hey, handsome," she greets the barista, voice bubbling over like champagne. "Hit me with the usual."

Everyone's grinning now, caught up in her wake, and I can't help but notice how she's like a damn sunray in this place. She's all warmth and light, weaving through the tables, leaving laughter trailing behind her like a scarf.

My hand stops its mindless path. Instead, I grip the mug tight, a lifeline in a suddenly too-bright world. I know this isn't my scene, but there's something about her—like a puzzle I want to solve or a code I need to crack.

Yeah, she's definitely got my attention.

I look away and internally chide myself. I have no business gawking over her. Hell, I don't even know her.

And that's what I'm doing when it happens. I'm trying my damndest to not look at her when a scalding wave of coffee crashes against my chest, seeping through the fabric of my shirt. The shock of it has me on my feet in an instant, coffee mug clattering to the table, a few splashes jumping out to mark the white surface like a crime scene.

"Shit! I am so, so sorry!" The pretty little brunette's voice is a frantic symphony, her hands fluttering in the air like wild birds. Her eyes are wide saucers of oh-my-god-what-did-I-just-do, and she's biting her lip in a way that should be illegal.

My skin prickles beneath the soaked shirt, anger and surprise warring for dominance. My jaw clenches as I peel the fabric from my skin, dark with wetness and damn uncomfortable. "It's fine," I lie through gritted teeth, my voice low and restrained. It's not fine. But what can I do? Unleash hell over an accident?

"Here, let me help." She's already pulling napkins from the holder, dabbing at the stain on my shirt like she's trying to erase the mistake. I catch her wrist, gentle but firm. "Don't."

"Really, I'm so embarrassed. Let me pay for your shirt or dry cleaning or...anything?" Her offer tumbles out in a rush, the words tripping over each other in their haste to make up for the disaster.

"Let it go." My fingers release her wrist, and I force a half-smile that doesn't quite reach my eyes. "Accidents happen."

She steps back, a flush creeping up her neck, painting her cheeks in shades of mortification. She's a mess of apologies, and damn if that doesn't soften the annoyance simmering in my gut.

"Can I at least buy you another coffee?" There's hope in her voice now, a tentative bridge extended across the chasm of our clumsy introduction.

"Sure," I relent with a shrug, watching as she turns to signal the barista, her hat still jauntily perched atop her head, as if it hasn't just witnessed the debacle.

I sit back down, rolling my shoulders to release the tension. The annoyance lingers, a bitter aftertaste, but there's something about those expressive brown eyes, that messy cascade of apologetic words, that hooks into me, refuses to let go.

"Another round on me," she says, sliding into the chair opposite mine. "And this time, I promise to keep the coffee in the cup."

"Promise, huh?" I drawl, the corner of my mouth twitching. Maybe it's the heat of the coffee still clinging to my skin, or maybe it's her, but I'm suddenly aware of every detail—the way her fingers curl around the mug, the quick dart of her tongue as she licks a drop of latte from her lip.

"Scout's honor." She crosses her heart, and I can't help but chuckle.

"I'm, Kelly, by the way," she introduces herself.

"Greg," I answer as I lean back to take her in. She's a splash of color in my gray world, unexpected and jarring, but not entirely unwelcome.

"Seriously, though, I'm a klutz, certified and everything." Her hands flutter like birds as she speaks, each movement punctuating her rapid-fire words. She's trying to make light of the situation, and her smile is like a damn sunrise in this place that smells more of burnt espresso than hope.

"Certified klutz? Is there a training course for that?" My voice is dry, but I can't deny that there's a twitch at the corner of my mouth.

Watching her animated display is like observing a different species—one that thrives on sunshine and sugar.

"Absolutely," Kelly says, her eyes twinkling with mischief. "I excel at tripping over flat surfaces and bumping into stationary objects. It's a gift." She tilts her head, brown locks tumbling from beneath her hat, which is frankly too stylish for a Tuesday morning.

"Sounds dangerous," I reply, keeping my tone even, but inside, I'm wary. This kind of free-spiritedness is foreign to me, and it scratches at the walls I've built around myself.

"Only to myself—and apparently, to unsuspecting bystanders like you." A giggle escapes her, and it's infectious, though I lock down the response before it can show on my face. "I promise I usually have better aim with my coffee."

"Good to know," I say, folding my arms across my chest—a barrier against more than just errant coffee spills. "So, what brings you here today? Besides redecorating strangers' shirts?"

"Work, actually." She pulls out a seat without asking and sits down, her presence suddenly filling the space opposite me. "I'm meeting a client here. I design things...graphics, websites, logos. You know, making the world prettier one pixel at a time."

"Ah," I nod, acknowledging the stark contrast between her creative flair and my own utilitarian view of the world. "Sounds fulfilling."

"Most days." She shrugs, then leans forward, resting her elbows on the table. "What about you? You seem more like a...well, not a graphic designer."

"Got that right," I agree. "I'm just grabbing coffee before heading to the gym. Routine keeps me grounded."

"Routine is good," she says quickly, almost tripping over her words in her eagerness. "But a little chaos can be fun, don't you think?"

"Fun isn't exactly the word I'd use," I tell her, thinking back on the years where chaos was the norm, where it meant life or death, not spilled coffee and laughter.

"Maybe not," she concedes, tapping a finger against her chin. "But it makes for a good story, right?"

"Depends on who's telling it." I stand up, feeling the itch to move, to put distance between me and this whirlwind of a woman who seems to see life as a thing to be celebrated rather than survived.

"Hey, before you go..." Kelly starts, but I hold up a hand.

"Keep your coffee aimed in the other direction next time, and we'll call it even," I say, offering her a tight-lipped smile that doesn't quite mask the twinge of regret for cutting this short. But some stains, like the ones on my shirt and the ones in my mind, need more than a quick cleanup—they need time and space, something I'm not ready to give.

I don't wait for her reply. I can't. Instead, I stride away, each step heavy with the things I don't say, the things I can't allow myself to feel. Not now. Not with her bright eyes and her easy smile that make me want things I have no right to want.

"Goodbye, Kelly," I whisper to the door as it closes behind me, sealing her off from me.

My curiosity about her festers, an itch I *won't* scratch. Not today. Maybe not ever.

CHAPTER
TWO

Greg

I'M AT MY LAPTOP, the soft glow of the screen casting shadows around my dimly lit room. I can't shake her from my mind—Kelly, with those expressive brown eyes that seem to see right through me. It's like a tickle in the back of my brain, an itch I just gotta scratch. So I do what I do best. I dive deep into the web, slipping past the usual crap on social media to find the real her.

My fingers fly across the keyboard with a precision that's second nature, honed in places where information means the difference between life and death. It doesn't take long before I've pieced together her schedule, her habits, the little tidbits that make up her day-to-day. There's a pang of something—guilt, maybe?—but it's drowned out by a surge of something else entirely as I click through her pictures.

There she is, laughing with a vibrancy that fills the pixels before me. Her style's all bright colors and confidence, hats tipped just so atop her long brown hair. I lean back, letting my mind wander, letting the fantasy take shape. My hand moves of its own accord as I unzip my pants and fist my hard cock.

I stroke it swiftly as I picture what it would be like to have her here with me. To hear those quick, excited words spill from her lips while my name rides on her breathy moans.

When my cum bubbles up from my tip, the release is sharp and sweet. A momentary escape that leaves me hollowed out and even more restless than before.

"Shit," I mutter, swiping a hand down my face. This isn't me, or at least, it shouldn't be. Stalking a woman online, getting off to a digital ghost—it's a line I never thought I'd cross. But with Kelly...hell, it feels like I don't have a choice.

I tell myself to stay away, to let whatever this

is fizzle out. But the next thing I know, I'm walking the streets, tracing her steps like some lovesick shadow. I know her favorite spots now, the rhythm of her life in this city. And it's no surprise, really, when I end up outside that same coffee shop, the one where we first met.

I tell myself I just want to see herself up close again.

I know it's a damn lie, though.

"Hey, stranger," greets that warm voice, knocking the wind clean out of me. She's there, looking every bit as radiant as she does in her online world, maybe more.

"Kelly." Her name's a reflex on my lips. "Fancy meeting you here."

"Total coincidence," she says, but her smile tells me she doesn't buy it any more than I do.

"Right," I say, matching her grin with one of my own. "Coincidence."

"Well, since you're here, I'm fixing to hit up an art exhibit. Would you like to come?" Her invitation is sudden, but it's warm and inviting and sincere, and my heart stutters in my chest.

How the fuck can I say 'no' to those pretty brown eyes?

So, I trail behind Kelly, my footsteps silent as a ghost's. We're in the art museum, surrounded by more beauty than I've known since my desert days. But it's her—Kelly, with her brown hair cascading down her back like a waterfall of silk, pondering over paintings with that look of wonder in her eyes. *She's* the masterpiece I can't stop studying.

"Monet's brushstrokes are just...orgasmic, don't you think?" Her voice pulls me from my reverie, a playful lilt dancing in her words.

"Orgasmic?" I chuckle, closing the distance between us. "That's one way to describe them."

"Look closer," she insists, her finger tracing the air near the canvas, careful not to touch. "It's like he made love to the canvas. Each color, each line —it's an intimate dance."

"Intimate." The word hangs heavy between us, loaded and dangerous. Like a grenade with its pin pulled.

She turns to face me, those expressive eyes locked onto mine. "Art is all about emotion, Greg. It's raw, exposed...vulnerable."

Vulnerable. She says it like it's something beautiful, not a weakness that could shatter you into a thousand irrecoverable pieces.

"Is that so?" I manage, my throat tight. We move through the gallery, shoulder to shoulder, but there's an ocean of unsaid things stretching out between us.

"Yeah," Kelly nods, her gaze lingering on a painting of lovers entwined. "It's...passionate."

"Passionate," I repeat, and she looks at me then, really looks at me. There's heat there, under the surface, simmering. My heart thuds against my ribcage, a staccato rhythm threatening to break me open.

"Let's grab coffee after this," she suggests, her voice a soft caress against the buzz of the museum.

"Sounds good," I agree, because coffee means more time with her, more chances to soak her in like the parched earth soaks in rain.

But as we walk, I can feel the familiar itch of my scars, the ghosts of a past life whispering in my ear. They're always there, lurking, waiting for a moment of weakness to drag me back to hell. I'm broken in ways Kelly can't see, haunted by memories that paint a far different picture than the ones on these walls.

"Greg?" Her hand brushes against mine, a jolt of electricity. "You okay?"

"Always," I lie, offering her a smile that doesn't quite reach my eyes. Because here's the thing—I *want* her. God, how I want her.

But there's a war inside of me, battles being fought every day and night, and I can't help but fear I might drag her into the trenches with me.

"Come on," she says, tugging me toward the exit. "I need that coffee."

"Lead the way," I say, and follow her out into the sunlight, trying to shake off the shadows that cling to me like cobwebs.

But even as we sit across from each other in the café, our laughter easy and conversation flowing like wine, I know I'm walking a razor's edge. Every moment with her is both agony and ecstasy, a reminder of everything I yearn for and everything I'm terrified to reach for.

Our knees brush under the table, an electric current passing between us with each accidental touch. Her eyes, warm and inviting, lock onto mine, and I can tell she's serious about peeling back my layers.

"Talk to me," she urges softly, her hand reaching across the table to lightly cover mine. "About anything. About everything."

I hesitate, feeling the weight of my past pressing down on me. But something in Kelly's gaze tells me it's okay to let go, to unravel before her. So I start talking, words spilling out of me like rounds from a chamber.

"The military...it was my life, you know? But out there—in the dust, the heat, the noise—it changes you." My voice is a low rumble, almost drowned out by the clinking of cups and the murmur of other patrons. "And coming back home, it's like you're a puzzle piece that doesn't quite fit anymore."

Kelly squeezes my hand, her thumb tracing circles on my skin. "But you're here now, Greg. With me. And I want to help you find where you fit, even if it takes a while."

Her words are a balm to the raw edges of my soul. And as I dive into the darker parts of my service—the fear, the loss, the relentless night-mares—I feel the walls I've built crumble brick by brick. She listens, not flinching at the horrors I describe, not judging the man who's been forged in the fires of war.

"PTSD is a tricky bastard," I confess, the confession scratching its way up my throat. "It sneaks up on you when you least expect it, stealing your peace, your sleep, your control."

"Then we'll fight it together," she says fiercely, her resolve sparking something within me. "You're not alone, Greg."

The vulnerability in her eyes mirrors my own, and I realize I'm done fighting this—fighting us. I lean forward, closing the distance between us until our lips are a breath apart.

"Kelly," I whisper, my heart thundering against my chest.

"Greg," she whispers back, a tremor in her voice.

Our mouths meet in a kiss that's both a promise and a plea, soft and slow at first, but growing deeper, hungrier. It's a collision of need and longing, a silent acknowledgment of the connection that's been simmering between us from the moment we met.

My hands find their way into her hair, tangling in the soft brown strands, pulling her closer. She responds with equal fervor, her arms wrapping around my neck, her body pressing against mine. The world shrinks until there's nothing but the taste of her lips, the sound of our mingled breaths, and the undeniable truth that we belong to each other.

"God, Kelly," I groan against her mouth, "I want you so much."

"Then have me," she breathes out, her desire a match to my own.

We leave the coffee shop and walk the short block to my apartment.

Neither of us speaks. I can't, and I'm afraid if I say anything it will break this moment.

I know better. I shouldn't do this. I'm at least ten years older than her and jaded from the military. She's too young and pretty and vibrant and carefree. I'll only taint her.

But god help me, I can't stop.

I pull her into my apartment and into my arms.

And then my lips are on hers again, my tongue slipping into her mouth.

She moans into the kiss, her hands pulling at my shirt, seeking skin. The feel of her fingers tracing fire across my chest shreds the last of my restraint. I lift her up without breaking our connection, and she wraps her legs around my waist, a perfect fit against my body.

We stumble into the bedroom, our movements desperate, fueled by a hunger that's been building since the first glance. As we fall onto the bed, clothes are shed without care, each piece a barrier we can't wait to destroy.

"Greg," she pants as I trail kisses down her neck, tasting the salt of her skin, "please."

Her plea is my undoing. My hands explore every curve, memorizing the landscape of her body as if it's a map to my salvation. When I find her hot and ready, the sound of her sharp intake of breath drives me wilder. I position myself at her entrance, looking into her eyes for any sign of hesitation.

There's none—just raw, unbridled desire.

I push into her slowly at first, giving us both time to adjust to the feeling of being connected so deeply. Her eyes flutter shut, lips parting in a silent cry of pleasure that sends shockwaves through me.

And then I go completely still when I realize she's unbelievably tight.

"Kelly, are you a virgin?" I look down at her in shock as she bites her lip and nods.

I close my eyes tight and try to control my breathing. *Mine!* She's all mine. *Only* mine.

"You beautiful, perfect thing," I groan out as I can't control myself anymore and start pumping in and out of her.

She whimpers, and I feel her pussy flutter around me, and that only drives me wilder.

"Fuck, baby, this little virgin cunt has got me going crazy, you know that? You know how perfect you are?"

Kelly doesn't speak. She simply cries out and clings to me as I fuck into her harder and harder.

With each thrust, I go deeper, both of us losing ourselves in the rhythm we create together.

Her legs tighten around me, pulling me in closer as she meets my movements with urgency. The room fills with the sounds of our breathing and the soft cries that spill from her lips each time I touch just right.

As we climb higher together, our bodies slick with sweat and need, Kelly's cries grow louder, more insistent. "Greg...I'm close," she gasps out.

Hearing her on the edge sends me reeling. "Yes, baby, that's it. Come for me. I'm right there with you."

With a few more thrusts, I follow her over, our climax tearing through us like a storm. I hold her tight as I flood my cum into her, my cock spasming harder than it ever has before.

Mine! This woman was made for me. It's all that goes through my mind as I mark her with my seed.

Lying there in the aftermath, Kelly's head on my chest and our limbs entangled, I feel a peace settle over me—a stark contrast to the chaos that usually reigns in my mind. Her fingers draw lazy circles on my skin as she plants soft kisses across my collarbone.

"I've never felt anything like that," she murmurs against my skin.

I tighten my hold on her. "Neither have I," I confess softly. For once not afraid to acknowledge the depth of what's happening between us. This isn't just physical—this is soul-deep, transformative.

Maybe for the first time since returning home from war-ridden lands, burdened with scars seen and unseen. Here in this quiet moment with Kelly —I dare to hope for something more permanent than fleeting peace. Maybe even something like happiness.

CHAPTER
THREE

Kelly

THE SEA BREEZE tangles through my hair, salty and wild, like the thoughts racing in my head. Beside me, Greg's presence is a steady beat, his steps sinking into the sand in sync with mine. The beach is our secret hideaway, untouched and intimate, perfect for what I hope might unfold between us.

"Looks like we've got the place to ourselves," I muse, sneaking a glance at him. His intense eyes are on the horizon, but I catch the corner of his lip twitching upwards in that half-smile that always sends my heart into a fluttery dance.

"Seems so," he replies, his voice deep and smooth as the ocean itself.

We choose a spot where the beach kisses the edge of the world, and I shake out the blanket with a flourish. It floats, then settles on the sand. We ease down onto it, careful, as if the space between us is something sacred.

I can't believe how quickly everything happened between Greg and me, but I wouldn't change any of it. We might be polar opposites, but there's something about the war vet that just tugs at my heart. He makes me feel seen and safe and I don't know…

The way he felt when he was inside me…I never knew it could feel that way. No wonder people like sex.

"Perfect timing," I say, nodding toward the sun that's beginning to dip low, painting the sky in hues of fire and passion. "It's beautiful."

"Nothing compared to you," Greg murmurs, and it's cheesy, sure, but it's also so earnest that it ignites a warm glow inside me. His compliment feels like a caress.

I draw my knees up, wrapping my arms around them, while Greg stretches out beside me, our bodies forming two pieces of a puzzle that just needs a little nudge to fit together. Our fingers brush, accidental-on-purpose, and an electric charge sizzles up my arm, delicious and promising.

"Sunsets always make me feel like anything's possible," I whisper, allowing my shoulder to lean a fraction closer to his.

"Anything?" His voice is a challenge, wrapped in velvet, tempting me to close the gap between us.

"Anything." My reply is a breath, a dare, a surrender all at once.

Greg's gaze lingers on my lips, and I can almost taste the kiss that's hanging in the air between us, sweet and spicy, calling us to indulge in its promise. But we don't rush. Not yet. Because sometimes, the buildup is just as exquisite as the release.

Instead, we sit together.

The sun dips lower, painting the sky a kaleidoscope of blush and amber. It's like nature's own seduction, coaxing every hidden desire to the surface, making my skin tingle with anticipation. Greg is beside me, close enough that I can feel the heat radiating from his body.

He takes a deep breath, his chest rising and falling with a weight that's about more than just air. His eyes, those intense pools reflecting the fiery horizon, lock onto the setting sun with a determination that sends a thrill through me. For a moment, he's a statue, all chiseled lines and quiet strength, a warrior gathering his courage before the battle.

Then, as if making some silent decision, Greg turns to me. The intensity in his gaze pins me in place, a raw display of nerves and need that I've never seen from him before. It's as if he's stripping himself bare, not of clothes, but of walls, and what's left is pure, unguarded Greg.

"Kelly," he breathes out, and damn, the way my name sounds on his lips should be illegal. It's husky, loaded with emotions that have no place being this exposed, this vulnerable.

My heart hammers against my ribcage, a frantic Morse code spelling out desire. I turn to meet his stare, feeling naked under the scrutiny, yet craving it all the same. My stomach flutters, a storm of butterflies set loose by his mere presence.

"Greg." My voice is a whisper, laced with every ounce of yearning that simmers beneath my skin. The air between us crackles with electricity, with words unsaid and touches unmade. I'm caught in his gravitational pull, helpless and entirely willing.

His eyes search mine, as if he's looking for an answer or maybe permission. In them, I see a man who's fought battles but now stands before me, fighting something far more intimate. And I know, whatever he needs to say, I'm here for it, ready to dive into the depths of his soul.

"Talk to me," I urge, my tone soft yet insistent, because understanding Greg, seeing all of him, feels essential—like breathing.

Greg's hand edges toward me, a slight tremor betraying his soldier's steadiness. His fingers brush against my cheek, and it's like a spark to dry tinder. Heat races down my spine, igniting every nerve ending into acute awareness.

"Kelly," he whispers, the sound rough like gravel, yet it caresses me in ways I didn't know possible. I lean into his touch, my skin hungry for more of his warmth, my body alive with a thousand unspoken promises.

"Greg," I breathe back, daring to close the gap between desire and reality.

And then we're kissing, his lips pressing urgently against mine, telling stories of longing kept at bay for far too long. It's a clash, a dance, a melding of two people starved for this very moment. His mouth moves over mine with a fervor that speaks of raw need, and God, do I need him too.

The world tilts, fades, becomes nothing more than background noise to the symphony of our combined breaths and the soft sounds of surrender. My hands roam over the hard planes of his chest, feeling the hammering of his heart through layers of muscle and bone.

His arms encircle me, strong and unyielding, drawing me closer until there's no space left for doubts or fears, just the searing connection of his body pressed against mine. This kiss is more than just an act of passion—it's a lifeline, a silent vow exchanged in the language of touch and taste.

"More," I gasp when his lips trail fire along my jawline, exploring territory that begs to be claimed. His response is immediate, a low growl that vibrates against my skin, sending shivers of anticipation to the very core of me.

I'm gasping for air, my heart racing like it's trying to break free when Greg's lips finally leave mine. He pulls back just enough to lock his intense gaze with mine, those deep-set eyes now swirling with a storm of emotions. His chest heaves, and I feel his breath, warm and ragged against my skin.

"Kelly," he starts, the timbre of his voice rough

around the edges, cracking under the weight of what he's about to say. "I've got these demons, shadows from my time at war. They don't just haunt me—they're part of me."

His admission hits me hard, right in the gut, but it's his vulnerability that slices through me, raw and unguarded. There's a tremor in his hand as it falls from my face, like he's laying down his last line of defense.

"PTSD. It's this...constant battle in my head. And I'm scared, so fucking scared that one day I might hurt you without meaning to." His words hang heavy between us, a confession laid bare by the dying light of the sun.

"Greg," I breathe out, my own voice shaky with the swell of emotions that threaten to over-flow. "You won't hurt me. You're the strongest person I know." I reach up, daring to trace the scar on his jaw, a stark reminder of the hell he's been through. "You've survived battles most can't even imagine. We'll fight this one together, too."

There's a fierceness in my vow, an unwavering determination that I hope he can feel. Because I mean every word—from the deepest, most stubborn part of my soul, I mean it.

"Supporting you isn't just something I'm willing to do, it's something I need to do." My fingers curl around his, squeezing tight. "I'm here, Greg. For all of it. The dark, the light, and every shade in between."

He searches my face, looking for the truth behind my words, and I let him see it—all the love, all the acceptance.

"Fuck, you beautiful girl, I love you," he finally groans out before he crashes his lips back onto mine.

And my soul soars. He loves me! I don't even get a chance to say the words back because his lips are trailing down my neck, leaving a rush of fire in their wake. All I can do is whimper and moan as our movements turn frantic.

He's pulling my dress up as he pulls me onto his lap and unleashes his cock from his pants. We're both still dressed enough that no one can see our nudity, but if anyone looked hard enough, it would be obvious what we're doing when Greg lowers me down onto his hard length and starts bouncing me up and down on him.

I wrap my legs around him, clinging to him as if he's the only thing keeping me grounded in this whirlwind of sensation and emotion. The rhythm we find is desperate, unapathetic to the setting sun or the encroaching night. It's just us, here and now, pulsating together in a frantic ball of need.

His hands are on my hips, guiding me, urging me on in a silent plea for more—always more. And I give it willingly, losing myself in the push and pull of flesh against flesh. The sounds of the ocean fade into a distant murmur, drowned out by the thrumming of our hearts and our labored breathing.

"God, Kelly," Greg grunts, his voice strained as he thrusts upward, driving deeper into me with each rise and fall of our bodies. His eyes are closed tight, creases forming at the corners as if he's trying to memorize this feeling, burn it into his mind where no shadow can reach.

The cool sand beneath us grows damp with the evening tide, but we're too lost in each other to care about the chill. I can feel him everywhere —not just physically but seeping into the spaces inside me that had too long been cold and vacant.

Suddenly, his grip tightens, a warning without words. I nod slightly against his shoulder, acknowledging what's to come. With a few more fervent moves, we're both tumbling over that edge, crying out against the rush of release that overtakes us. His name spills from my lips like a prayer as wave after wave crashes through me, leaving behind nothing but satisfaction and soul-deep contentment.

As our breaths even out and our grips loosen slightly, Greg presses his forehead against mine. "I didn't know...I needed this," he whispers hoarsely.

"I did," I whisper back with a gentle certainty as I stroke his hair back from his forehead—a small gesture that feels deeply intimate in its simplicity.

We sit there for a moment longer under the cloak of twilight—the world holding its breath around us—as we memorize this perfect imperfection. Finally pulling my dress down and helping Greg adjust himself back into his pants, we laugh softly at our disheveled state.

I lean back against the worn blanket, feeling the coarse sand shift beneath its thin fabric, and let out a long breath. The sky blushes with the colors of an impending nightfall, and there's a kind of beautiful stillness that wraps around us— a rare moment of peace in our otherwise chaotic worlds.

"Greg," I murmur, my voice barely louder than the hush of the sea breeze, "what scares you the most about...everything?"

He shifts beside me, his body language open yet tense, like he's preparing to lay bare his soul. "Losing control," he admits, his gaze piercing the horizon. "Not just with PTSD, but in life. I'm used to structure, orders, knowing the next move. Civvy street doesn't come with a manual." His laugh is humorless, a puff of air that dissipates quickly into the salt-laden wind.

"Join the club." My attempt at lightness doesn't quite mask the tremor in my words. "Design might seem all fun and colors, but it's like I've got this judge inside my head, always telling me I'm one step away from screwing up big time."

"Your work is brilliant, Kelly," he says, turning to face me, his voice firm. "You capture stories in your design, make them speak without words."

My cheeks heat up, and it's not from the sun's dying rays. It is Greg—always Greg—who sees through the facade to the frightened girl scribbling on the walls, desperate to be heard.

"Maybe," I whisper, the confession feeling like a boulder lifted off my chest, "but I'm scared it'll never be enough. That I'll never be enough."

"Enough for what?" His hand finds mine, fingers lacing together instinctively, as natural as drawing breath.

"Life, love, success—the whole damn package."

"Kel," he starts, then stops, his brow furrowing. He looks like he's battling some internal war before he finally speaks again. "What if we take control back? Together."

A shiver races through me, because it's not just his words—it's the promise in them. "What do you mean?"

"Let's create something. Something that merges the chaos of my past with the beauty of your art. We can tell a story, make sense of things." His voice grows stronger, surer, as if the idea gives him a foothold in this slippery slope we're both on.

"Like a project?" The word tastes like adventure on my tongue, a shared secret that's ours alone.

"Yeah. A project." His eyes light up, and it's like I can see the gears turning in his mind. "We could start with a historical series, bring those silent heroes to life, and you—you could design the hell out of it."

"Greg," I breathe out, stunned, excited, alive. "That's...that's bloody brilliant."

"Only if you're in," he says, squeezing my hand.

"Of course, I'm in." My heart pounds with a rhythm that's all anticipation and desire—for the project, for the man who came up with it, for the future we might just carve out together. "Let's do this."

"Let's do this," he echoes, and the smile that stretches across his face is one of the purest things I've ever seen. It's a smile that speaks of hope, of dreams taking flight, and just like that, I'm soaring right alongside him.

CHAPTER
FOUR

Greg

I'M SPRAWLED out on the bed, my muscles wound tight as a coiled spring. Eyes wide in the dark, I stare at the ceiling that's just a shade lighter than pitch black. The quiet's too loud, suffocating, filled with whispers of doubts that crawl through my mind like unwelcome intruders. I push against the sheets, restless, as fears gnaw at the edges of my consciousness—fears of closeness, of that raw vulnerability that comes with letting someone in.

"Fuck," I mutter to myself. The idea of being in a relationship, it's like dancing on a minefield.

Every step could be the one that blows it all to hell. Memories, sharp and unbidden, slice through me—the weight of responsibility, the crushing loneliness, the scars that no one sees but feel like they're on display every damn second. Kelly...she deserves someone whole, not this fractured mess of a man.

A shiver runs down my spine as sleep tugs at me, dragging me down into its depths. I resist, knowing what waits for me there. But it's no use. I'm pulled under, and everything goes from murky to crystal-fucking-clear terror.

Now I'm back there, in the dust and the heat and the screams. My rifle's in my hands, heavy and real, and I'm running, always running. Smoke blurs my vision, but I can see them—my brothers-in-arms, fallen, faces contorted in pain and shock. And there's nothing I can do, nothing but fight and pray and survive.

"Greg, move your ass!" someone yells, but the voice is distant, drowned out by the ringing in my ears. Bullets zip by like deadly hornets, and my heart's slamming against my ribcage like it's trying to break free. Each breath is ragged, tearing through my throat, but there's no air, only the taste of fear and gunpowder.

"Help me..." It's a whisper, a plea, and I know

that voice. I turn, but he's not there, just the ghost of a memory, eyes pleading from behind a blood-soaked bandana. No matter how fast I move, I can't reach him, can't save him. Powerless. Fucking powerless.

And then I'm falling, the ground ripped away beneath my feet, and I'm yelling, screaming until my voice is raw. But it's not enough. It's never enough.

"Kelly..." Her name rips from my throat, a lifeline in the chaos, but she's nowhere, just a dream within a nightmare. And the thought of her, waiting in the world beyond, safe and warm, it's the cruelest cut of all. Because here, in this hell, I'm alone. Utterly alone.

———

Panting. Drenched in sweat like I've just run a goddamn marathon. My heart's a sledgehammer against my chest, trying to burst through skin and bone. It's the dead of night, but the darkness is no sanctuary—it's a fucking prison.

"Shit," I gasp out, throwing the tangled sheets off my overheating body. I can't shake the images, the sounds. They cling to me, a second skin of terror. And Kelly...I look down at her still sleeping soundly, thank god. But fuck, I could've hurt her. The thought alone strangles me, coils of guilt tightening around my throat until I can barely breathe.

"Get it together, Greg." It's a whisper to myself, but it echoes like a shout in the silence of my room. I swing my legs over the edge of the bed, feet hitting the floor with a dull thud. Each step feels like wading through molasses as I pace, back and forth, a caged animal in a too-small enclosure.

"Can't do this to her. Can't risk it," I mutter under my breath. Every instinct screams to pull her close, to feel her warmth, her pulse beneath my fingertips. But memories are cruel masters. They whip and lash, painting every touch with shades of fear.

I stop by the window, hands pressed against the cool glass. The moon's a voyeur, its pale light casting long shadows across the room, across my body.

"Damn it!" The words tear from me, raw and ragged. I clench my fists until my nails bite into my palms, the pain a welcome distraction from the chaos inside my head. Kelly deserves better than a broken man with a head full of nightmares.

"I'll keep you safe, even if it means staying the hell away." The vow tastes like ash. It's a promise drenched in sorrow, a sentence self-imposed. But I'll bear it. For her, I'll shoulder this loneliness, this ache that carves hollows in my chest.

"Fuck," I groan, running a hand through my hair. It's not what I want. It's the last damn thing I want. But it's the only play I've got. Because I won't be the monster in her story. Not ever.

So, I slip out while she's asleep.

I've got to do the right thing even if it tears my heart in two.

———

I tap the screen of my phone, a quick slide to refresh. Her profile pops up—the same one I've been lurking on for days. The soft glow illuminates the dark room, casting shadows that flicker like the doubts in my head. She's smiling in her latest post, looking radiant as ever, and my chest tightens. It's just an image, but it feels like a punch straight to the gut.

"Fuck," I mutter under my breath, thumb hovering over the heart icon. I want to reach out, to tell her everything, but there's this beast inside me, clawing at my insides, whispering that I'm no good for her. I can't press it. I can't let her know I'm here, watching, wanting. So, I just look, the images a silent film of her life without me.

She tried to contact me, but I refused to answer my phone. She got the hint, and I can imagine the hurt on her beautiful face, but she has to understand I'm doing this for her own good, and if I see her now, I'll cave.

And then I might accidentally hurt her.

And I can't have that. *Won't* have that.

A photo of her at our favorite café pops up, and the memory of her laugh, bright and genuine, hits me. My finger twitches, and there it is—an accidental like. Shit. Panic rises like bile. I quickly undo it, hoping she doesn't notice. But what if she does? What if she thinks I'm some kind of creep?

"Get a grip, Greg," I chide myself, locking the phone before I make another mistake.

The room feels too small suddenly, trapping me with the echo of my own thoughts. I stand, muscles stiff from tension, and start pacing. Back and forth. Back and forth. The worn carpet under my bare feet is a path to nowhere.

Avoid—must avoid. The mantra plays over in

my head. Don't go where she might be. Don't risk seeing her face, those eyes that see too much. I skip the morning run we used to do together, dodge the park where she sketches. Even the damn grocery store feels off-limits now. I choose loneliness over the ghost of her presence, haunting every corner of this godforsaken town.

"Pathetic," I scoff at my reflection in the window, nothing but a shadow against the night. "You're a fucking coward."

The bar down the street buzzes with life, laughter spilling into the night air. Once, I would've been there, maybe with her, sharing jokes and stealing kisses. Now, the idea of being around people, their questions, their pitying looks—it's too much. So, I turn away, retreat back into the darkness of my apartment, my cell.

"Better alone," I whisper, sinking into the couch, letting silence swallow the space. "Better for everyone."

My phone sits there. One more peek, one last glimpse before I shut it all out. But I know that road, where it leads—to more pain, more regret. So, I leave it be, a small act of defiance against my own twisted desires.

"Tomorrow," I tell myself, "maybe tomorrow

I'll be stronger." But as sleep comes to claim me, dragging me down into dreams I don't want to face, I know it's just another lie. Tomorrow is just another day without her, another day fighting this war within.

CHAPTER
FIVE

Kelly

I STALK the length of my room, back and forth, like some caged animal. The walls close in, taunting me with memories. Enough is enough. I need to see him, need to hear it from his lips— why he's shut me out, why he's left me alone in this confusion that cuts deeper than any knife.

"Greg?" I call out, knocking on his door, my heart thrashing against my ribs. "We need to talk."

I can almost hear the grit of his teeth grinding on the other side. The door swings open, and there he stands, a brooding statue framed by the doorway. His eyes, those intense pools of torment, don't quite meet mine.

"Kelly." His voice is a low rumble, a storm brewing on the horizon. He doesn't step aside, doesn't welcome me in. "Now's not a good time."

"Like hell it isn't," I shoot back, pushing past him into the dimly lit space that smells of him, of us. "You've been avoiding me, Greg. Ghosting me like I'm some one-night stand. What did I do? Tell me."

"Kelly, you don't understand—" he starts, but I cut him off.

"No, you're right, I don't!" My voice rises, a crescendo of hurt. "I thought we had something real, something worth fighting for. Was it all just bullshit?"

"Watch your mouth, Kelly," he warns, the edge in his voice sharper than I've ever heard. But I'm past caring, past being the nice girl who waits quietly.

"Or what, Greg? You'll leave me again?" I spit the words at him, venomous and dripping with accusation. "Go ahead. Run away from this, from us. It's what you're good at, isn't it?"

His jaw clenches, muscles working beneath the stubble that lines his face. "You think I want to be this way? You think I enjoy pushing you away?" He steps closer, and I can feel the heat radiating off his body. "Every night, I fight demons you can't even imagine, Kelly. And I won't let them touch you. Can't you see? I'm fucked up, beyond repair."

"Stop using your past as an excuse to act like an asshole!" I'm screaming now, tears blurring my vision. "Everyone has scars, Greg. But you...you use yours to build walls instead of bridges."

"Damn it, Kelly! You're too good for me, too pure, too alive." His voice breaks, and it's like I can see the cracks in his armor. "I'm a disaster waiting to happen. A grenade with the pin pulled out."

"Then let me be your bomb squad," I plead, reaching for his hand, desperate to bridge the gap between us. But he recoils as if burned.

"No." The word is final, a gunshot in the silence. "It's over, Kelly. For your own good. Leave."

"Fine." The sobs rack my body, but I straighten up, anger giving me strength. "Have it your way, Greg. But when you're lying here alone, remember this. I loved you, despite everything. And you threw it away."

I storm out, letting the door slam behind me, a punctuation mark to the end of us. As I walk away, my heart shatters with each step, pieces scattering like shrapnel. We were supposed to be explosive together, not apart. But in the end, he was right—we were a disaster. And now, we're just wreckage.

———

Greg

The door slams shut behind her, and I'm alone—more alone than I've been in a long fucking time. The echo of it bounces around the sparse room like my own thoughts, ricocheting off the walls until I can't stand it. I press my palms into my eyes until I see stars, but it doesn't stop the ache in my chest.

"Fuck," I mutter to the empty room, the word hollow, useless. My heart's a clenched fist, every beat a pulse of raw hurt, reminding me she's gone. Kelly's gone because I pushed her away, because I couldn't be the man she needed. The man she deserved.

I stumble through days that blend into nights, haunted by the memory of her—her laugh, her touch, the way her brown eyes lit up when she smiled. It's like a goddamn curse, feeling her absence like a missing limb. I drown myself in workouts, pushing my body until it screams, anything to silence the chaos in my head. But nothing works. She's there, a ghost in every corner of my life.

It's on one of those endless nights that the call comes. A lifeline thrown into the churning sea of my self-made solitude. Mike's voice is a gruff reminder of a past life, one where brotherhood meant something more than blood.

"Greg, you stubborn son of a bitch," he growls through the phone, and even though it's been years, his voice is a slap of reality. "I've been hearing things, man. You're spiraling. You need to get your shit together."

"Mike, I—" What? Have excuses? Can justify how fucked up I am? I got nothing.

"Listen to me," he interrupts, all drill sergeant now. "You survived hell. Don't let it claim you now, not when you're home, not when you have a shot at happiness."

"Kelly's gone," I confess, the words tasting like defeat. "I'm toxic, Mike. Everything I touch—"

"Is bullshit," he snaps. "You think you're the

only one with demons, brother? We all got 'em. But we fight, Greg. That's what we do."

His words hit hard, a punch to the gut that knocks the wind out of me. Fight. It's what I know, what I'm trained for. But this battle, it's different—it's against an enemy that knows all my secrets, my weaknesses. Myself.

"Get help, Greg. For the PTSD, for whatever else is eating you up inside. Do it for yourself, or do it for her. But do it." Mike's voice softens. "You deserve more than this. And so does she."

When the line goes dead, the silence isn't as oppressive as before. It's almost...expectant. Like the universe is holding its breath, waiting for me to make a move. To fight back.

"Okay," I whisper to the darkness. "Okay."

It's a start, a tiny spark in the night.

———

Kelly

I'm slumped on the couch, scrolling mindlessly through my phone when the doorbell rings. My heart does that stupid leap thing it always does, like a pathetic Pavlovian response, hoping it's Greg. But no, it's just me being an idiot because I know who's on the other side of that door.

"Hey," Jenna says as she breezes in, her arms laden with what looks like half the grocery store. "Thought you could use some reinforcements."

"Chocolate and wine?" I guess, trying for light-hearted but landing somewhere closer to bitter.

"Among other things." She gives me that look, the one that says 'I'm here for you, spill it'.

"Jen," I start and then stop. How do you tell your best friend that your heart feels like it's been through a shredder?

"Kell, you're amazing. You know that, right?" She doesn't wait for my nod. "You're talented, you're gorgeous, and any guy would be lucky to have you."

She's laying it on thick, bless her. The thing is, all I can think about is how none of that seemed to matter to Greg.

"Greg's...he's got his own stuff, you know? It's not about you."

"Feels pretty personal when you get dumped because you're too much to handle," I mutter, picking at a loose thread on the cushion.

"Kelly," Jenna says firmly, grabbing my hand

with her surprisingly strong grip. "You are not too much. You are enough. More than enough. And if Greg can't see that, then he's the one missing out."

I want to believe her, I really do. So, I nod, swallowing around the lump in my throat. "Yeah."

"Besides," she continues, "you've got your work. Your art. That's part of who you are, and it's incredible. Focus on that. Grow from this. Because no man should define your worth."

Her words are like a cold splash of water, shocking me out of my pity party. She's right. I'm a graphic designer extraordinaire. I can't let Greg —or the lack of him—turn my life upside down.

"Okay," I say, more to myself than to her. "Okay."

That night, after Jenna leaves, I sit at my drafting table and lose myself in lines and colors, shapes and shadows. It's therapeutic, pouring everything I feel into something tangible. I'm good at this. Damn good.

And maybe, just maybe, that's enough for now.

———

Greg

Across the city, in the small hours where everything seems possible or hopeless depending on your brand of insomnia, I'm sitting on the edge of my bed, a man wrestling with ghosts.

"Fight," Mike had said. And fight I shall.

I reach for my phone, hands shaking—not with fear this time, but with something like determination. I punch in Kelly's number, staring at it like it's a grenade pin.

"Hey," I whisper into the voicemail, her bright, cheery greeting a stark contrast to the gravel in my voice, "it's Greg. I...fuck, I'm sorry. For everything. I'm getting help, Kel. For the PTSD. For us, if you'll still have me."

The words hang there, naked and raw in the silence of my room. It's done. Ball's in her court.

I don't know if she'll call back, if those bridges are ash or just a little scorched. But hope, that treacherous, beautiful thing, starts to unfurl in my chest, a stubborn green shoot pushing through the cracks in the concrete.

Maybe it's foolish. Maybe it's brave. But it's a start. And right now, it's all I've got.

CHAPTER
SIX

Greg

THE DOOR CLICKS SHUT behind me, a soft echo in the empty space of Dr. Marshall's office. I'm here again—same time, same place—but something feels different today. The weight on my chest isn't as crushing. Maybe it's because I've finally decided to stop running from the chaos in my head.

"Greg, how has your week been?" Dr. Marshall asks, her voice smooth like the jazz playing low in the background.

"Better," I confess. "I dusted off those old project files Kelly and I were working on."

"Good to hear," she nods, tapping her pen against her notepad. "And how does that make you feel?"

"Like I'm taking back control." The words come out stronger than I expect. It's the truth. Working on the project with Kelly...it was the first thing that made sense when I got back from hell overseas.

Dr. Marshall smiles, encouraging. "That's progress. Remember, healing is a journey."

Yeah, a freaking marathon. But for the first time, I feel like I might actually reach the finish line. We dive into the gritty stuff then—the memories that claw at my insides, the nightmares that drench my sheets. It's raw, it's real, but I don't shy away. Not this time.

Later, I'm at my desk, fingers flying over the keyboard when my phone buzzes. A message from Mike. He's been a good friend throughout all of this.

"Kelly's design won the pitch. It's brilliant," it reads.

A surge of pride swells in my chest. That's my girl—always doubted herself, but damn, she's got talent that could set the world on fire. And I've been a fool to let my demons keep me from her light.

I stand there, staring at the screen. Kelly's recognized her worth, and hell, it's about time I recognize mine too. She's the one I want beside me, the one who makes all the shadows recede. And I'm done letting my past hold me back from our future.

———

I push open the door to the coffee shop, the scent of roasted beans hitting me like a welcome slap in the face. The place is buzzing with life, but my eyes zero in on her immediately—Kelly, sitting at our old table, fingers twisting a lock of hair.

She stills whens she sees me. Her eyes widen, and her lips part slightly.

"Greg," she breathes out as I approach, and that one word is laced with so many emotions it nearly knocks the air from my lungs.

"Kelly." My voice feels rough, unpracticed, but it's full of everything I haven't been able to say.

We stand there for a moment, the world blurring into insignificance around us. Then, as if pulled by some magnetic force, we collide, her body slamming into mine with an urgency that leaves no space for doubt or hesitation. Her arms wrap around my neck, my hands find the small of her back, and we cling to each other like we're the only solid things left in a spinning universe.

"God, I've missed you," I whisper against her hair, inhaling the familiar scent of strawberries and something uniquely Kelly.

"Me too. So much," she says, her voice muffled against my chest.

We pull back just enough to see each other's faces, and that's when the apologies start tumbling out, clumsy and heartfelt. "I'm sorry for shutting you out," I say, the words feeling like shards of glass in my throat.

"And I'm sorry for pushing too hard," she counters, her brown eyes shimmering with unshed tears.

"Let's just...let's just be there for each other, okay? Fully, without holding anything back," I propose, desperate for her to understand.

"Deal." She nods, and in her eyes, I see the reflection of my own resolve.

"Full disclosure then," she begins, biting her lip. "Your demons scare the hell out of me sometimes, but they're part of you. And I love all of you, Greg. Even the broken bits."

"Jesus, Kelly," I say, a laugh bubbling up because she's just so damn perfect in her honesty. "You know how to knock a guy off his feet."

She grins, that infectious smile that could light up the darkest corners of my mind. "Only if he's wearing combat boots."

"Smartass." I chuckle, shaking my head in disbelief. How did I get so lucky?

"Love you, Greg" she whispers, and the world tilts again, but this time in the best possible way.

"Love you more," I reply, and it's not just words. It's a vow, a promise etched deep into my soul.

We lean in, our lips meeting in a kiss that's sweet and fierce all at once, sealing our declaration. When we part, her forehead rests against mine, and I swear I can feel the strength of our bond pulsing between us like a living thing.

And it's been too long because my cock is a leaking sieve in my pants.

"Kelly, baby, I need you," I rasp out as I press myself against her.

Her little gasp lets me know she gets my message. She takes my hand and leads me to a back corner of the coffee shop where she opens a closet and pulls me inside.

And I don't even give a fuck that we might get caught. As soon as that door shuts, I slam her against the wall and pull her thighs up.

Her breath catches, a mix of excitement and

urgency sparking in her eyes. "Greg," Her voice is a husky whisper that drives me wild.

"Can't wait," I growl back, my hands roaming over her body with a hunger that's been pent up too long. My fingers trail down the curves of her hips, gripping her tighter to me. The close confines of the closet amplify every sound, every breath—a cacophony of desire.

She wraps her legs around my waist. "Me either," she moans as she teasingly bites her lip.

I capture her mouth with mine, our tongues tangling in a dance as old as time but as electrifying as if it's our first kiss. My hand finds the hem of her skirt, pushing it up, searching for the warmth between her thighs. She moans into my kiss, a sound that stirs deeper lust within me.

I break away from our kiss just long enough to look into her eyes. "Hold tight," I whisper before diving into the crook of her neck, kissing, nibbling, marking her as mine. She tilts her head back against the wall, giving me better access, her hands fisting in my hair.

The scent of coffee beans and pastries fades into the background, replaced by the intoxicating aroma of her arousal mingling with mine. I free myself from my jeans with one hand—the other still securing Kelly to me—and position myself at her entrance.

"Greg," she breathes out as I push into her, filling us both with an exquisite pressure. Our confined space doesn't allow for much movement, but it's enough. Each thrust is sharp and deep, driven by months of longing and desire.

Her fingertips dig into my shoulders, anchoring herself as she meets each of my movements with fervor. The soft thuds against the closet walls are drowned out by our synchronized gasps and moans. Everything is intense, concentrated—our pleasure building rapidly towards an inevitable edge.

"Kelly," I rasp out through clenched teeth as I feel that familiar climb beginning in the pit of my stomach.

"Me too," she whispers back, eyes locked on mine as we spiral together into that blissful oblivion. I come with a muffled roar. I slam my hand over Kelly's mouth just in time to muffle her scream that would have surely given us away.

Moments later, we're leaning against each other for support in the aftermath, breathing heavily. She kisses me gently—so tender it makes my heart ache with love.

We fix ourselves up quickly but don't rush to

leave our makeshift sanctuary. Instead, we stay there for a minute longer than necessary, wrapped in each other's arms.

Stepping out finally into the light of the coffee shop again feels like coming back from another world. We share a quiet smile—our little secret—and return to our table as if nothing happened.

Yet everything has changed—we're solid now. Unbreakable. And I know no matter what shadows lie in wait for us outside these walls, together we can face anything and emerge stronger.

With Kelly by my side, I'm ready for anything. My girl is worth fighting for.

EPILOGUE

One year later

Kelly

I ADJUST the lighting one final time, stepping back to admire our work. The exhibit gleams under the soft luminescence, each piece a testament to months of labor, love, and a little bit of luck. Around us, the museum buzzes with visitors, but it feels like it's just Greg and me in our own little world.

"Looks amazing, doesn't it?" I say, sweeping my gaze over the digital canvases we've created together.

Greg nods, his eyes reflecting pride and something deeper, something that warms my insides. "Couldn't have done it without you," he says, his voice steady but I catch the flicker of emotion there. He's not one for grand speeches, but his few words always hit deep.

"Likewise," I reply, bumping my shoulder against his. He grins, and I swear my heart does a somersault. Who knew a former soldier could have such a disarmingly sweet smile?

We walk through the gallery hand-in-hand, weaving between installations that tell stories of bravery, loss, and new beginnings. It's our story too, in a way. His past meets my designs, creating a narrative that speaks without words.

"Remember when you said you couldn't draw a straight line?" I tease, stopping in front of a graphic that melds his precise, tactical insight with my artistic flair.

"Still can't," he chuckles, the sound rumbling through his chest. "But I've got you to make my ideas look good."

"Always," I affirm, squeezing his hand. It's more than just the exhibit. It's a promise for all the tomorrows we'll face together.

"Think we've got a future in this?" Greg asks, his question laced with hope and a hint of vulnerability. The man who's faced down danger now looks to me for a different kind of courage.

"Definitely," I respond without hesitation. My past insecurities fade away when I'm with him. "As long as it's you and me, the possibilities are endless."

The exhibit hums around us, alive with visitors and whispers of appreciation, but all I see is the man beside me—the one who's taught me strength comes in many forms, including letting someone else into your heart.

We're in the quiet corner of the exhibit, the soft hum of hushed conversations fading as we slip behind a partition designed by yours truly. Greg leans me back against the cool surface, his hands tracing the silhouette of my hips with a familiarity that sends shivers up my spine.

"Kelly," he murmurs, his breath hot against my neck, "this...us...it's everything."

My heart races, the sound drowning out any remaining murmur of the crowd. "You're everything," I manage to get out, my voice barely above a whisper.

His lips find mine, insistent and fiery, stoking a need deep within me that only he can satisfy. I tangle my fingers in his short-cropped hair, pulling him closer as if I could somehow meld us together. There's a hunger in his kiss, one that speaks of a passion that's both raw and achingly sweet.

"Want you," I breathe against his mouth, and that's all it takes.

He looks into my eyes, those intense depths that have seen too much yet still gaze at me like I'm the center of his universe. "Here?" he asks, a hint of that measured, deliberate manner seeping through despite the urgency in his touch.

"Here," I confirm, emboldened by desire and the thrill of being surrounded by our success—the exhibit that tells a story of overcoming the past and embracing the future.

Greg smiles wickedly and falls to his knees in front of me. I suck in an intake of breath as he puts his head under my dress and pushing my panties to the side.

And then I feel his tongue licking me.

I hold onto his shoulders.

My knees weaken as waves of pleasure crash through me. Greg's touch is electric, skilled, every move calculated to draw out the deepest moans that I struggle to keep hushed. The hum of the gallery fades to a distant murmur, drowned out by the rapid beating of my heart and the slick heat building between us. I can't it. I begin riding his face, seeking more of the pleasure only my husband can give me.

His hands grip my hips, pulling me closer, urging me on. I feel every bit of the rough texture of his callused hands, reminding me just how much this man has been through, how much he's faced. And yet here he is, worshipping me with fervor reserved only for those who have truly battled through darkness.

"Greg," I gasp, my fingers digging into his shoulders. The partition shields us from prying eyes but adds an exhilarating sense of daring to our escapade. His tongue flicks more insistently, and I feel that familiar climb, the coiling tension that threatens to snap.

I look down at him, his intense gaze locked on mine, dark and full of desire. It's a look that says he's not just here for release but for connection, for something that transcends the physical pleasure we're giving each other.

Suddenly I'm there, tumbling over the edge with a silent scream and a cascade of shudders. Greg guides me gently through it, his hands steadying me as I quake under his touch. Finally, he rises to his full height and kisses me deeply, sharing the taste of my surrender on his lips.

"My turn," I tell him as I fall to my knees and slip his cock out before he can protest.

I take him deep into my mouth until I feel his cock hit the back of my throat.

Greg groans, his hands finding their way to my hair, guiding me with a gentle urgency. The roughness of his fingers interwoven in my strands is both raw and intimate, a tether that connects us beyond words.

I look up at him, seeing the way his eyes close with the sensation, how his jaw clenches, a warrior undone by pleasure. It's powerful, this ability to unravel such a man, to watch him surrender under my touch. I increase the pace, driven by the desire to give him as much bliss as he has given me.

His breathing becomes ragged, punctuated by deep, guttural noises that resonate through the quiet partition. The thrill of our secret encounter mixes with the fear of discovery, heightening every sensation. Our world narrows down to just the two of us and the electric connection sparking between our bodies.

"Kelly," he breathes out, his voice strained with need. "I'm close."

I double my efforts, drawing him deeper, feeling

him swell in response. And then he's there—his body stiffens, and he gives himself over to the ecstasy with a low growl that vibrates through his chest. I savor him, the taste of him mingling with the rush of power and affection flooding through me.

Gently easing back as he recovers, I stand and we share a slow, deep kiss that speaks of gratitude and love more than any words could. "You're amazing," he murmurs against my lips.

"And you," I reply with a soft smile, "are everything I ever wanted."

We adjust ourselves quickly as we hear footsteps approaching. Slipping back into our public personas just in time, we step around the partition hand-in-hand, faces flushed with more than just triumph over our exhibit's success.

As we mingle back among the guests admiring our work, I can't help but feel a profound sense of completion. This project was not just about our professional talents melding. It was also about discovering the depths of our personal commitment and desire.

We receive compliments and congratulations on the exhibit's impact and design from several visitors who note an almost palpable energy in our displays. Little do they know how much of ourselves—our challenges and triumphs—has infused this space.

As the evening winds down and we prepare to leave, Greg pulls me close for one final look at our creation. "This is just the beginning," he promises with a confident smile that reaches deep into his eyes. "I'm going to give you the world, baby."

"Just you is enough," I tell him.

And I mean it.

Want a free book from Emma Bray? Go to www. authoremmabray.com.